It's Bedtime, Cucuy!
¡A la cama, Cucuy!

By / Por Claudia Galindo

Illustrations by / Ilustraciones de Jonathan Coombs
Spanish translation by / Traducción al español de John Pluecker

PIÑATA BOOKS

Piñata Books
Arte Público Press
Houston, Texas

Publication of *It's Bedtime, Cucuy* is funded by grants from the City of Houston through the Houston Arts Alliance, the Clayton Fund, and the Exemplar Program, a program of Americans for the Arts in collaboration with the LarsonAllen Public Services Group, with funding from the Ford Foundation. We are grateful for their support.

Esta edición de *A la cama, Cucuy* ha sido subvencionada por la Ciudad de Houston por medio del Houston Arts Alliance, el Fondo Clayton y el Exemplar Program, un programa de Americans for the Arts en colaboración con LarsonAllen Public Services Group, con fondos de la Fundación Ford. Les agradecemos su apoyo.

Piñata Books are full of surprises!
¡Piñata Books están llenos de sorpresas!

Piñata Books
An Imprint of Arte Público Press
University of Houston
452 Cullen Performance Hall
Houston, Texas 77204-2004

Galindo, Claudia, 1979-
  [It's Bedtime, Cucuy. English & Spanish]
  It's Bedtime, Cucuy / by Claudia Galindo; Illustrations by Jonathan Coombs; Spanish translation by John Pluecker = A la cama, Cucuy / por Claudia Galindo; ilustraciones de Jonathan Coombs; traducción al español de John Pluecker.
      p.   cm.
  Summary: Cucuy does everything he can think of to avoid going to bed in this rhyming story told in Spanish and English.
  ISBN 978-1-55885-491-8 (alk. paper)
  [1. Bedtime—Fiction. 2. Behavior—Fiction. 3. Monsters—Fiction. 4. Spanish language materials—Bilingual.] I. Title: A la cama, Cucuy. II. Coombs, Jonathan, ill. III. Pluecker, John, 1979- IV. Title.
PZ73.G1418 2008
[E]—dc22
                                                          2008007576
                                                          CIP

∞ The paper used in this publication meets the requirements of the American National Standard for Permanence of Paper for Printed Library Materials Z39.48-1984.

8 9 0 1 2 3 4 5 6 7   10 9 8 7 6 5 4 3 2 1

For all of my wonderful teachers who inspired me to keep telling my stories and to my students who I hope will continue telling theirs.
—CG

To my wife for her love and support and to my son
for bringing us joy.
—JC

Para todos mis maravillosos maestros quienes me inspiraron a contar mis historias y para mis estudiantes quienes espero que continúen contando las suyas.
—CG

Para mi esposa por su cariño y apoyo y para mi hijo
por traernos alegría.
—JC

Cucuy is a little monster that doesn't like to sleep.

Every night at bedtime he screams and kicks his feet.

El Cucuy es un pequeño monstruo al que no le gusta dormir.

Cada noche grita y da patadas a la hora de acostarse.

"I'm not sleepy!" he says as he tries to sneak away.

"All I want to do is jump around and play!"

—¡No tengo sueño! —dice, mientras trata de escapar.

—¡Sólo quiero jugar y saltar!

He makes ugly faces and tries to hide in all of his favorite places.

Hace muecas y trata de esconderse en sus lugares favoritos.

Even in all that craze Mamá is able to put him in his pj's.

En todo el alboroto, Mamá logra ponerle su piyama.

He wiggles and jiggles hoping that Mamá will give in, but she will not let him win.

Se menea y se sacude esperando que Mamá se canse, pero ella no lo deja ganar.

"Shhhh . . ." Mamá says. "Close your little eyes."

"It's not fair!" shouts Cucuy and begins to cry.

—Shist . . . —dice Mamá—. Cierra los ojitos.

—¡No es justo! —grita el Cucuy y se pone a llorar.

He pulls his hair, oh what a sight, hoping to win this bedtime fight.

Se tira el pelo, uy qué feo, tratando de ganar esta pelea.

He mumbles and grumbles all sorts of excuses . . .

"I'm hungry, I'm thirsty. I've got to go potty."

Murmura y regaña con muchas excusas . . .

—Tengo hambre, tengo sed. Tengo que ir a hacer pipí.

And then he stands up and declares:
"I won't go to sleep!" he says with an ugly stare.

Y entonces se para y declara:
—¡No voy a dormir! —dice con una fea mirada.

"Now that is enough fuss," says Mamá and tucks him in with loving care.

—Ya basta —dice Mamá y lo arropa con cariño.

"But why do I have to go to bed?" asks Cucuy as his face turns red.

—Pero, ¿por qué tengo que acostarme? —pregunta el Cucuy con la cara bien roja.

"Because you need to rest," Mamá whispers in his ear. "Tomorrow you will have a whole new day to jump around and play."

—Porque necesitas descansar —Mamá le susurra en el oído—. Mañana podrás saltar y jugar todo el día.

Cucuy makes more ugly faces as he thinks about hiding in his favorite places. He wiggles and jiggles and then mumbles and grumbles until he finally . . .

El Cucuy hace más muecas y piensa en esconderse en sus lugares favoritos. Se menea y se sacude, después murmura y regaña hasta que por fin . . .

. . . says, "Okay, maybe if I count some
sheep I can get
just
a
tiny
bit
of . . .
sleep . . . "

. . . dice: —Bueno, quizás si cuento ovejas,
podría darme
un
poco
una
pizca
de
sueño . . .

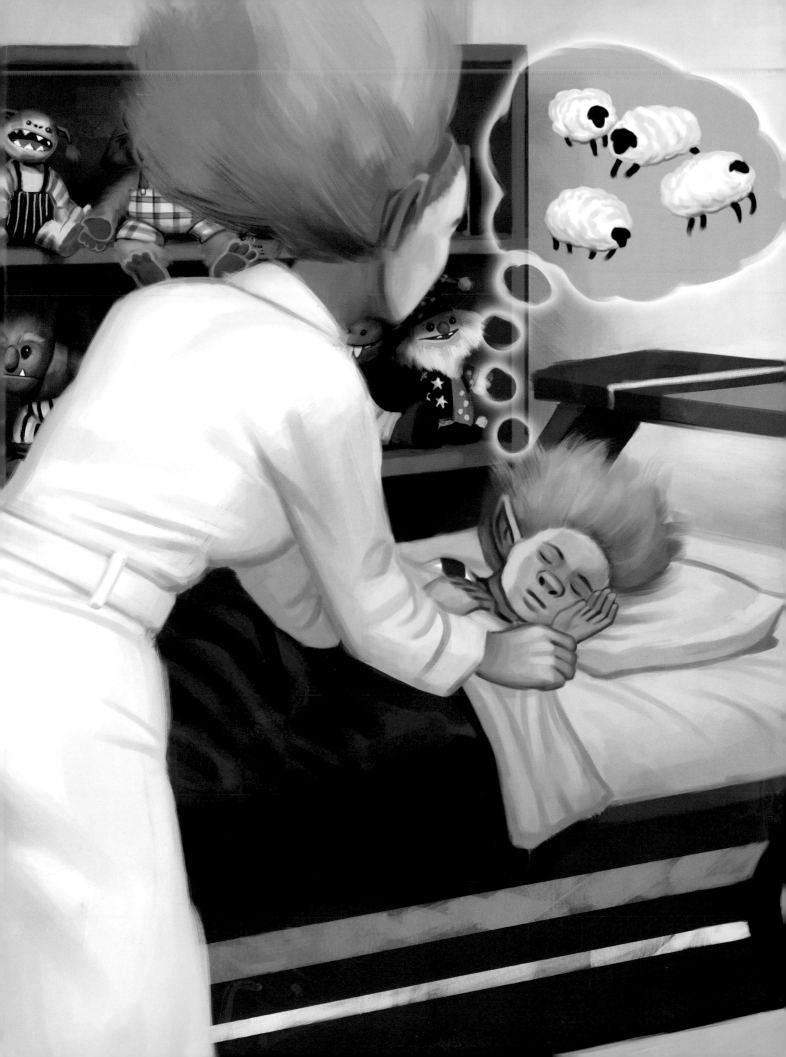

Claudia Galindo, the author of *Do You Know the Cucuy? / ¿Conoces al Cucuy?* (Piñata Books, 2008), attended the University of North Texas, where she received a degree in Journalism and a Masters in Education. She is currently a teacher in Dallas, Texas, where she lives with her two children.

Claudia Galindo, autora de *Do You Know the Cucuy? / ¿Conoces al Cucuy?* (Piñata Books, 2008), recibió una licenciatura en periodismo y una maestría en educación de University of North Texas. En la actualidad es maestra y vive en Dallas, Texas, con sus dos hijos.

Jonathan Coombs is the illustrator of *Do You Know the Cucuy? / ¿Conoces al Cucuy?* (Piñata Books, 2008). He lives with his wife and son in Utah, where he works as an artist at a video game studio and does various freelance illustration projects.

Jonathan Coombs es el ilustrador de *Do You Know the Cucuy? / ¿Conoces al Cucuy?* (Piñata Books, 2008). Vive con su esposa y su hijo en Utah y trabaja como artista en un estudio de juegos de video y como ilustrador independiente.